SiR
RYAN'S
QUEST

SiR RYAN'S QUEST

Jason Deeble

A NEAL PORTER BOOK
ROARING BROOK PRESS
NEW YORK

Copyright © 2009 by Jason Deeble

A Neal Porter Book

Published by Roaring Brook Press

Roaring Brook Press is a division of Holtzbrinck Publishing Holdings Limited Partnership

175 Fifth Avenue, New York, New York 10010

Distributed in Canada by H. B. Fenn and Company, Ltd.

Cataloging-in-Publication Data is on file at the Library of Congress

ISBN-13: 978-1-59643-330-4

ISBN-10: 1-59643-330-2

Roaring Brook Press books are available for special promotions and premiums.
For details, contact: Director of Special Markets, Holtzbrinck Publishers.

Printed in China

Book design by Jennifer Browne

First edition April 2009

2   4   6   8   10   9   7   5   3   1

For my mother,
Barbara Deeble

Ryan crawled into the kitchen cupboard one morning while still wearing his pajamas. Today, he was on a quest.

The pots bumped and banged
against each other. Outside, Ryan
could hear his mother cleaning
up from breakfast.

"Right this way, Ryan," said a spaghetti pot. "The king has been expecting you."

"Sir Ryan," said the king of
pots. "You are a brave knight.
I will assist you on your quest."

"Take this armor and find what you seek in the jungle on the mountain."

And then, in his new suit of
armor, Sir Ryan began his quest.

He scaled the great mountain,

until he came to the deep, dark jungle,
where the air was thick and heavy,
and vines fell all around him.

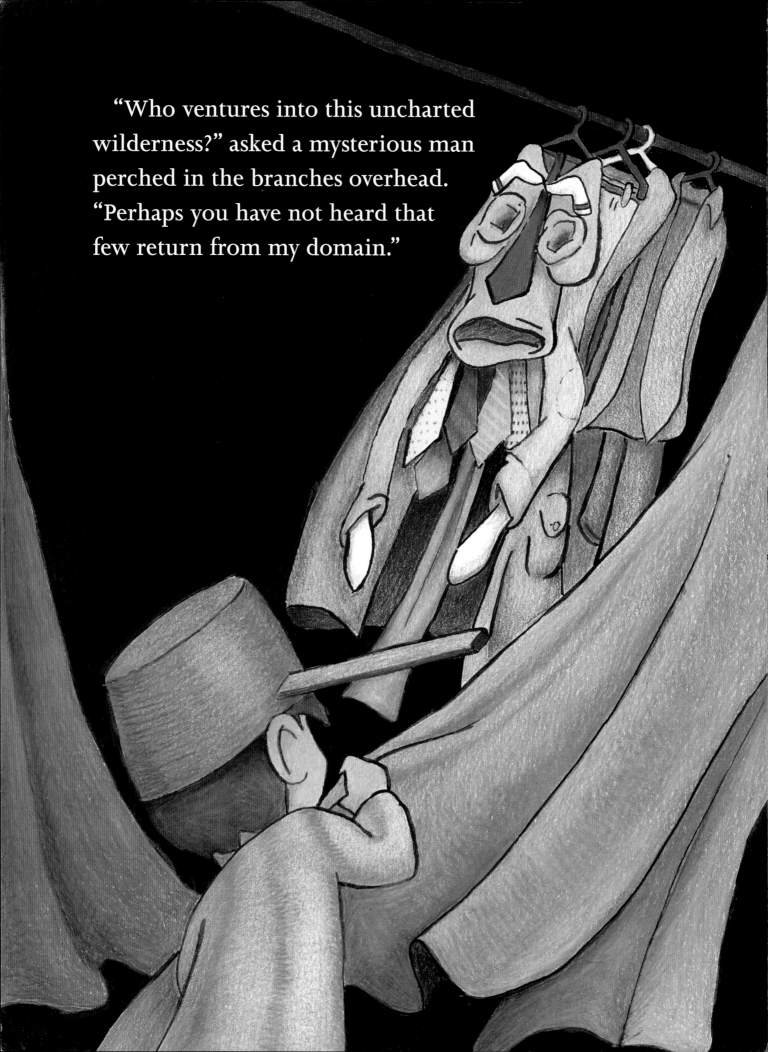

"Who ventures into this uncharted wilderness?" asked a mysterious man perched in the branches overhead. "Perhaps you have not heard that few return from my domain."

Said Ryan: "I am not afraid. His Majesty, the king of the pots, has given me this suit of armor to keep me safe. I ask only for your help so that I may complete my quest."

"You are a brave knight," said the mysterious man. "You must visit the castle at the foot of this mountain, but before you go, take with you this enchanted cape. All who see it will know my magic is with you on your quest."

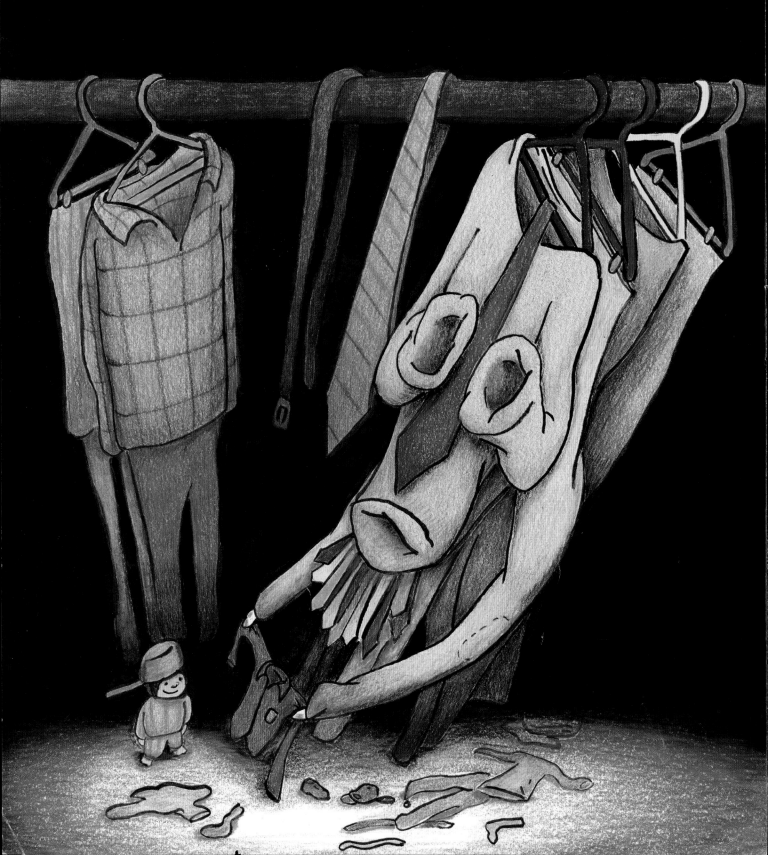

Sir Ryan thanked the mysterious
man and climbed back down the
mountain to find the castle.

Beyond the castle gates,
Sir Ryan saw oily machines
piled high on every side.

"Are you friend or foe?" asked the castle guard, steely and square. "None shall pass unless they have honorable intentions."

Said Ryan: "My intentions are indeed honorable, good sir. I am Sir Ryan and I am on a quest. Look upon my enchanted cape and know that I have faced great danger to visit your castle today."

"You are a most gallant knight," said the guard. "You must go into the cave beneath the kingdom to find what you seek, but before you go, take with you this shield. It will keep you free from harm."

Sir Ryan thanked the guard and left
to find the entrance to the cave.

The mouth of the cave was dark and dank.
Sir Ryan felt afraid, but he knew that a knight
must be brave. Down he went into the darkness.
Hand over hand, inch by inch, step after step.

In the cave beneath the kingdom, Sir Ryan found a moldy monster lurking in the shadows. "Who has dared to come into my cave?" it asked in a low groan. "Perhaps it is a meaty morsel for my lunch."

Said Ryan: "Mighty beast, I'm afraid my shield would be too much for you to stomach. Maybe, rather than eat me, you could help me on my quest."

"Though I am hungry, I could never eat such a brave knight," sighed the boxy beast. "I will help you on your quest. What you seek is not here. You must leave this cave, but before you go, take with you this sword and use it wisely. It will protect you on your quest."

Ryan thanked the beast and then,
hand over hand, inch by inch, step after
step, he climbed out from the cave.

Outside of the cave,
in the bright light of day,
he heard his mother.
"Where have you been, Ryan?"

Proudly he answered, "I am Sir Ryan and I have been on a quest! I met a king, climbed a mountain, explored a jungle, visited a castle, and went down into the deepest, darkest cave."

"Oh, you are a very brave knight," said his mother.
"A royal banquet will be held in your honor."

She prepared his feast,

and gave him a hug,

and Sir Ryan knew he had completed his quest.